CRICTOR

Story and pictures by TOMI UNGERER

SCHOLASTIC BOOK SERVICES

NEW YORK · TORONTO · LONDON · AUCKLAND · SYDNEY · TOKYO

For Nancy, Ursula and Susan

ISBN: 0-590-08030-X

Copyright © 1958 by Jean Thomas Ungerer. This edition is published by Scholastic Book
Services, a division of Scholastic Magazines, Inc., by arrangement with Harper & Row, Pub-
lishers, Incorporated.

21 20 19 18 17 16 15   1 2 3 4 5 6/8

Printed in the U.S.A.

07

Once upon a time in a little French town

lived an old lady whose name was Madame Louise Bodot.

She had one son who was in Africa studying reptiles.

One morning the mailman

brought her a peculiar O-shaped box.

Madame Bodot screamed when she opened it.

It was a snake her son had sent her for her birthday.

To make sure it was not a poisonous snake,

she went to the zoo. She identified it as a boa constrictor.

So she called her animal Crictor.

Madame Bodot mothered her new pet,
feeding it bottles of milk.

She bought palm trees so Crictor would really feel at home.

As dogs do when they are happy, he wagged his tail.

Well fed, Crictor grew longer and longer and stronger and stronger.

The boa followed his mistress when she went shopping.

Everyone was astonished.

Madame Bodot knitted a long woolen sweater
for her pet to wear on cold days.

Crictor also had a warm, comfortable bed.

There he would dream happily, under his palm trees.

In the winter it was fun for Crictor to wriggle in the snow.

Madame Bodot taught at the public school.

One day she decided to take Crictor to her classes.

Soon Crictor learned to shape the alphabet in his own way.

S as in snake

e as in elephant

N as in nothing

O as in oak

as in lion

as in man

as in glass

as in whale

He could count too, forming figures.

 for your two hands

 for the three little pigs

 for the four legs of the dog

5 for your five fingers

6 for the six legs of a bug

7 for the seven dwarfs

8 for the eight arms of the octopus

The boa liked to play with little boys

and little girls too.

He helped the boy scouts learn knots.

Crictor was a helpful snake.

One day in a sidewalk cafe Madame Bodot

heard from a friend at the next table that

there had been a series of thefts in the town.

That very night the burglar broke into her apartment.

Madame Bodot was already gagged and tied to a chair when the faithful boa awoke and furiously attacked the burglar. The villain's terrified shrieks awoke the neighbors.

Crictor remained coiled around him until the police arrived.

For his bravery a nice medal

was awarded to the heroic snake.

Crictor even inspired the local sculptor to make a statue in his honor.

And the city dedicated a park to him.
Loved and respected by the entire village,
Crictor lived a long and happy life.

The End